Naughty Nancy

By Anne Cassidy

Illustrated by Desideria Guicciardini

Special thanks to our advisers for their expertise:

Adria F. Klein, Ph.D.
Professor Emeritus, California State University
San Bernardino, California

Susan Kesselring, M.A.
Literacy Educator
Rosemount-Apple Valley-Eagan (Minnesota) School District

PICTURE WINDOW BOOKS
Minneapolis, Minnesota

Levels for *Read-it!* Readers

- Familiar topics
- Frequently used words
- Repeating patterns

- New ideas
- Larger vocabulary
- Variety of language structures

- Challenges in ideas
- Expanded vocabulary
- Wide variety of sentences

- More complex ideas
- Extended vocabulary range
- Expanded language structures

A Note to Parents and Caregivers:

Read-it! Readers are for children who are just starting on the amazing road to reading. These beautiful books support both the acquisition of reading skills and the love of books.

The RED LEVEL presents familiar topics using common words and repeating sentence patterns.

The BLUE LEVEL presents new ideas using a larger vocabulary and varied sentence structure.

The YELLOW LEVEL presents more challenging ideas, a broad vocabulary, and wide variety in sentence structure.

The GREEN LEVEL presents more complex ideas, an extended vocabulary range, and expanded language structures.

When sharing a book with your child, read in short stretches, pausing often to talk about the pictures. Have your child turn the pages and point to the pictures and familiar words. And be sure to reread favorite stories or parts of stories.

There is no right or wrong way to share books with children. Find time to read with your child, and pass on the legacy of literacy.

Adria F. Klein, Ph.D.
Professor Emeritus
California State University
San Bernardino, California

First American edition published in 2005 by
Picture Window Books
5115 Excelsior Boulevard
Suite 232
Minneapolis, MN 55416
877-845-8392
www.picturewindowbooks.com

First published in Great Britain by Franklin Watts, 96 Leonard Street,
London, EC2A 4XD

Printed in the United States of America.

Library of Congress Cataloging-in-Publication Data
Cassidy, Anne.
Naughty Nancy / by Anne Cassidy ; illustrated by Desideria Guicciardini.
p. cm. — (Read-it! readers)
Summary: Norman has his hands full when his mother tells him to take care of his little
sister Nancy as they take a walk on their farm.
ISBN 1-4048-0558-3 (hardcover)
[1. Brothers and sisters—Fiction. 2. Behavior—Fiction. 3. Farm life—Fiction.]
I. Guicciardini, Desideria, ill. II. Title. III. Series.
PZ7.C26857Nau 2004
[E]—dc22   2004007328

Norman had to look after his little sister, Nancy. She was the naughtiest girl he knew.

"I'm going out now," said Mom.
"Don't let Nancy frighten the sheep,
upset the hens, or bother the pigs!"

"Make sure she doesn't get into trouble, and try to keep her clothes clean!" she added.

Norman was not happy.

Norman took Nancy outside into
the yard. He showed her the
trees and the flowers.

"Look at this pretty red rose,
Nancy," he said.

But Nancy was already chasing
the hens.

"No!" shouted Norman. He ran into the henhouse after Nancy and caught her just in time.

Norman took Nancy to see the fishpond. He showed her the goldfish and the slimy frogs.

But Nancy wasn't looking.

She was trying to jump across the
stepping stones to the other side.

13

"No!" shouted Norman, splashing into the water.

Norman caught Nancy just in time.

He also caught some fish and a
slimy frog!

Norman was wet and fed up.
"Let's go into the sunshine and
play hide-and-seek in the
meadow," he said to Nancy.

Norman counted slowly to 100.
But Nancy wasn't playing.

Nancy was trying to count
the sheep. The sheep weren't
pleased at all.

Norman ran after Nancy and tried to catch her. But he just got in the way!

Norman took Nancy for a long walk in the woods. He took his nature book with him and showed her a beautiful blue butterfly. But Nancy wasn't looking.

Nancy wanted to catch her own
butterfly and climbed up a tree.

"No!" shouted Norman as he climbed up the tree after her.

But Nancy had jumped down.

24

Norman wasn't so lucky.

The branch broke, and he fell to the ground and landed in a bush.

On the way home, Norman and
Nancy passed the pigpens.
Nancy wanted to look inside.
She opened the gate.

Norman tried to close the gate,
but it was too late—the pigs came
trotting out!

They pushed past Norman, and he
fell in the mud.

"I've had enough!" shouted Norman.

"We're going straight home."

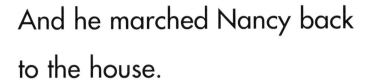

And he marched Nancy back
to the house.

Mom was very pleased.

"What a good girl you are, Nancy. Your clothes are clean, and your hair is neat and tidy."

"What a shame about your brother!" she added.

"In the future, I think I'll call him naughty Norman!"

Levels for *Read-it!* Readers

Read-it! Readers help children practice early reading
skills with brightly illustrated stories.

Red Level: Familiar topics with frequently used words and
repeating patterns.

I Am in Charge of Me by Dana Meachen Rau
Let's Share by Dana Meachen Rau

Blue Level: New ideas with a larger vocabulary and a variety
of language structures.

At the Beach by Patricia M. Stockland
The Playground Snake by Brian Moses

Yellow Level: Challenging ideas with an expanded vocabulary
and a wide variety of sentences.

Flynn Flies High by Hilary Robinson
Marvin, the Blue Pig by Karen Wallace
Moo! by Penny Dolan
Pippin's Big Jump by Hilary Robinson
The Queen's Dragon by Anne Cassidy
Sounds Like Fun by Dana Meachen Rau
Tired of Waiting by Dana Meachen Rau
Whose Birthday Is It? by Sherryl Clark

Green Level: More complex ideas with an extended vocabulary
range and expanded language structures.

Clever Cat by Karen Wallace
Flora McQuack by Penny Dolan
Izzie's Idea by Jillian Powell
Naughty Nancy by Anne Cassidy
The Princess and the Frog by Margaret Nash
The Roly-Poly Rice Ball by Penny Dolan
Run! by Sue Ferraby
Sausages! by Anne Adeney
Stickers, Shells, and Snow Globes by Dana Meachen Rau
The Truth About Hansel and Gretel by Karina Law
Willie the Whale by Joy Oades

A complete list of *Read-it!* Readers is available on our Web site:
www.picturewindowbooks.com